Skippy and Jack

by Patsy Backx

Gareth Stevens Publishing
A WORLD ALMANAC EDUCATION GROUP COMPANY

Jack was a clever young man.
He worked at the railroad station.
He liked his job, and he worked very hard,
but dancing was his inspiration.

At work on the platform, while mopping or sweeping,
young Jack was constantly kicking and leaping.

And as trains were leaving the station each day,
Jack blew on his whistle and danced a jeté.

He whirled and he twirled, from morning 'til night.
His ballet and tap were so graceful — so light.
As his co-workers watched him, you'd think they'd be proud.
Instead, they just whispered and pointed and scowled.

One day, his co-workers told Jack, "Enough!
We're sick of your whirling and twirling and stuff.
We're tired of your tiptoeing, prancing, and leaping.
Stop all this dancing! Get back to your sweeping."

For a while, Jack stopped.
He just didn't dare.
Then, one day, carting baggage,
he leaped through the air.

No sooner had poor Jack's
two feet left the ground
than his co-workers grabbed him
and pulled him back down.

The next thing Jack knew, he was riding the rail
in a car that was loaded with sacks full of mail.

The train rolled on for hours, then stopped at a town
where Jack leaped from that mail car
with one graceful bound.

Now, in that very town, Skippy, a dog,
lived with a man and his wife.
But Skippy was all alone most of the time.
He didn't fit into their life.

"Now, Skippy," they said, on that very day.
"We're leaving this town, and we're moving away.
We can't take you with us. It's sad, but it's true."

"You'll be on your own, now, so, go away! Shoo!"
Poor Skippy just didn't know what he should do.

So the man and his wife, I'm sorry to say,
tied Skippy outside — and just walked away.

Skippy sat there alone, half hidden by trees,
watching and waiting for somebody — please.

When who should pass by,
himself quite alone,
but our own clever Jack,
a long way from home.

Jack saw the poor puppy tied up to a tree
and thought to himself — hmm, now that shouldn't be!

"You poor little pup," Jack said with a tear.
"Are you all alone? Well, don't worry. I'm here."

Jack untied the leash
and stroked Skippy's head.
"Here, watch me! I'll dance
for you, doggie," he said.

Jack stood on one toe,
took a leap, did a spin.
Skippy jumped with delight,
so Jack did it again.

And then guess what happened.
The dog started dancing!
A crowd gathered around them.
The show was entrancing.

One man who was watching stepped forward to say,
"You can dance at my theater. Please, start today!"

Who would have thought? Who'd ever guess
that Skippy and Jack would be such a success?

They still dance together. They're very well-known.
And they've opened a theater all of their own.
Now dancing with Skippy is Jack's inspiration.
They're Skippy and Jack — the dancing sensation!

SKIPPY AND JACK THEATER

Please visit our web site at: www.garethstevens.com
For a free color catalog describing Gareth Stevens Publishing's
list of high-quality books and multimedia programs, call
1-800-542-2595 or fax your request to (414) 332-3567.

Library of Congress Cataloging-in-Publication Data

Backx, Patsy.
    [Verhaal van Stippie en Jan. English]
    Skippy and Jack / by Patsy Backx.
        p. cm.
    Summary: A young man, whose fellow railway workers do not appreciate his dancing
on the job, encounters an abandoned dog and together they become a theatrical sensation.
    ISBN 0-8368-3080-6 (lib. bdg.)
    [1. Dance—Fiction.   2. Dogs—Fiction.   3. Stories in rhyme.] I. Title.
PZ8.3.B133Sk   2002
[E]—dc21   2001054220

This North American edition first published in 2002 by
Gareth Stevens Publishing
A World Almanac Education Group Company
330 West Olive Street, Suite 100
Milwaukee, Wisconsin 53212 USA

This U.S. edition © 2002 by Gareth Stevens, Inc. Text and illustrations © 1993 by Patsy Backx.
Original edition published as *Stippie en Jan* © J.H. Gottmer/H.J.W. Becht bv, The Netherlands,
a Jenny de Jonge book.

English text: Dorothy L. Gibbs
Cover Design: Eva Erato-Rudek

Printed in the United States of America

1 2 3 4 5 6 7 8 9 06 05 04 03 02